STAND UP

AF198898

An English play in 8 scenes about MORAL COURAGE

For Years 8, 9 and 10 (Level 4/1)

By John Middleton

Bibliografische Information der Deutschen Nationalbibliothek:
Die Deutsche Nationalbibliothek verzeichnet diese Publikation
in der Deutschen Nationalbibliografie; detaillierte
bibliografische Daten sind im Internet über http://dnb.dnb.de
abrufbar.

Herstellung und Verlag: BoD – Books on Demand, Norderstedt

ISBN: 9783751918183

Other plays from THE PLAYLET SERIES by John Middleton:

EVERY DAY – a play in 10 scenes about EVERYDAY LIFE
for Years 2, 3 and 4 (Level 1/1)

FRIENDS – a play in 9 scenes about FRIENDS
for Years 3, 4 and 5 (Level 2/1)

NEW KEY CHAIN – a play in 15 scenes about KEYS
for Years 6, 7 and 8 (Level 3/1)

LUCKY CHARMS – a play in 10 scenes about LUCK
for Years 6, 7 and 8 (Level 3/2)

FEAR – a play in 7 scenes about FEAR
for Years 9, 10 and 11 (Level 5/1)

MONOLOGS FOR YOUNG ADULTS – 25 scenes
for Years 11 and 12 or for university students (September 2020)

<u>CONTENTS</u>

FOREWORD

STAND UP is a play for students in Years 8, 9 or 10 (Level 4/1). It is designed for a normal-sized English class and for students with varying interests in acting. Since there are 41 roles – none of which are really minor – students who enjoy acting can perform in several scenes and play to their heart's content, whereas students who aren't particularly keen on acting only have one role to master in one single scene. Every scene deals in a very special way with the question of moral courage and the many challenges young people face in our modern world when it comes time to stand up for what is right. There are monologues, dialogues and scenes with as many as eight or nine performers. The themes are geared to extreme situations which confront students nowadays – such as peer pressure, cyber-bullying and gender-related bullying, exploitation, unprovoked violence, self-destruction and rejection – and offer young actresses and actors the opportunity to discover a wide range of relevant dramatic topics and expression while performing. The plots are believable and understandable, the language is idiomatic and easily accessible for English learners. STAND UP works well when performed for smaller audiences: parents and other classes. But it can also be highly entertaining for a large audience. Performing time: about one hour. Of course, it is also possible to select individual scenes and perform them as simple skits outside the context of STAND UP. In that case it is still recommendable to create a suitable setting for presenting the skits to an audience. The true joy of performing a foreign-language play is to feel it click, to realize that the people watching the performance don't only "get the picture", they are also delighted to see a story come to life when presented in English by non-native performers.

– John Middleton, Hamburg, 2019

SCENE 1   OWN IT

(Patricia is on her way to school. She crosses the stage and stops at center stage. She pauses for a moment, then turns to address the audience. In the background – stage right – a boy, Paul, is sitting on a bench reading.)

PATRICIA

I'm scared… I'm on my way to school… It's a normal school day, this is a normal road in a normal town, I'm a normal schoolgirl, and I'm scared… So what am I scared of?... Well, let me tell you, this is the 21ˢᵗ century, so there are no wild animals that might attack me. There are no savages or pirates that might torture me or throw me to the sharks. There is no real physical danger I might be scared of. But I'm scared.

(Two girls, Jan and Liv, approach Patricia from stage right. Liv stops beside Patricia. Jan walks past Patricia, stops and turns to face her.)

LIV

Hey, Patty, I saw you in the Special Education room yesterday with all the retards.

JAN

Oh really? With all the retards? So that means you're a retard, too?

PATRICIA

During my lunch break I work with kids who have disabilities.

JAN

You work with retards and cripples? How disgusting!

LIV

I just thought you were a nerd – which is bad enough. But that you spend your lunch breaks with all the dumdums…

JAN

You know, Liv, it all kinda makes sense now. Her baggy clothes…

(Jan tugs at Patricia's sweater.)

LIV *(pulling Patricia's hair)*

And her greasy hair.

JAN

And her body odor!

(Jan holds her nose with one hand and waves her other hand as if fanning away the stench.)

LIV

That girl really stinks like a retard.

PATRICIA

Don't call them retards. They are special children with special needs, children with disabilities.

LIV

The only special need they have is the need to get a good shower.

JAN

Like you.

(Jan takes the bottle of water she is holding and pours it over Patricia's head. Jan and Liv laugh.)

LIV

She looks like a drowned rat now.

JAN

You mean a drowned retard.

LIV

Like I always say, the only good retard is a drowned one.

(The two girls laugh as they walk away. Patricia looks at the audience and raises her arms in disbelief. Suddenly Emma, Kellie and Amber walk past Patricia and then start circling her. Patricia watches them. After having been circled twice she looks down.)

PATRICIA

Hi.

(The three girls stop and laugh for a moment. Then they continue to walk around Patricia.)

PATRICIA

I haven't seen you guys for a while.

(Emma, Kellie and Amber stop in their tracks.)

EMMA

Did you say something?

AMBER

I didn't hear anything. In fact, all I see is one big NOBODY.

EMMA

Hey, that ain't nobody. That's Fatty Patty!

(Emma, Kellie and Amber chuckle.)

PATRICIA *(pleading)*

C'mon, guys. Stop messing around. What have you been up to?

(Emma, Kellie and Amber start circling Patricia again... once, twice, then they all stop behind Patricia and look over her shoulder.)

EMMA

Know what?

(She eyes Patricia from head to toe.)

At least there's one good thing about your body. It isn't as ugly as your face.

PATRICIA

What are you talking about?

KELLIE *(making fun of her question)*

"What are you talking about?"

AMBER *(shoves Patricia)*

You know damn well what we're talking about, bitch!

EMMA *(also shoves Patricia)*

You know that Kellie's going with Kyle, right?

AMBER *(grabs Patricia's shoulders from behind and shakes her)*

So why did you call him?

PATRICIA

I wanted to ask him about the topic for our essay in English and...

KELLIE

Bullshit!

EMMA

You were just trying to hit on him! Admit it, you slut!

PATRICIA

No way. We're just friends.

KELLIE

Just friends? Listen here, bitch.

(Kellie pulls Patricia's hair from behind.)

If you ever so much as look at Kyle again, you're one dead slut!
Understand?

*(Kellie lets go of Patricia's hair. Patricia steps forward to distance
herself from Emma, Kellie and Amber.)*

PATRICIA *(talking with her back to the other girls)*

Hey Kellie. There's nothing between Kyle and me. We've
known each other since we were little kids. Our families are
real close and…

*(Emma, Kellie and Amber walk in front of Patricia and stand next to
each other with their backs to the audience.)*

EMMA

Hey bitch! Didn't you get the picture?

AMBER

We're absolutely serious!

KELLIE

You're one dead slut.

*(Emma, Kellie and Amber all turn around at once – as if doing a
dance routine – and face the audience.)*

AMBER *(pulls her index finger across her neck to simulate cutting
someone's throat)*

Ahhhh!

KELLIE *(raises her fist next to her head to simulate hanging
someone)*

Ugh!

EMMA *(holds her hand up like a pistol, points her index finger at her head and simulates shooting someone)*

Bang!

AMBER

Have a nice day, sweetheart!

EMMA

But not in this world!

KELLIE

In other words, GET LOST.

(The three girls chuckle and leave. Patricia looks at the audience and raises her arms in disbelief. At the same time we hear one, two, three different ringtones. Three boys – Brad, Justin and Keanu – appear in the background as they cross the stage and stop at a distance of three feet from each other, standing in a straight line.) Each boy answers his phone. Patricia continues to stand in front of them, listening to everything they say.)

JUSTIN *(on the phone)*

Hey Amber…

KEANU *(on the phone)*

Hey Emma…

BRAD *(on the phone)*

Hey Kellie…

JUSTIN *(on the phone)*

You mean Fatty Patty?

KEANU *(on the phone)*

What about her?

BRAD *(on the phone)*

You gotta be kidding. She called Kyle?

JUSTIN *(on the phone)*

I thought Kellie was going with Kyle.

KEANU *(on the phone)*

There's no way Kyle would ever go out with her.

BRAD *(on the phone)*

C'mon, Kellie. There's nothing to worry about.

JUSTIN *(on the phone)*

Don't be stupid, Amber. Patricia is such a nerd.

KEANU *(on the phone)*

Listen Emma, I'll talk to Kyle, okay?

BRAD *(on the phone)*

Hey Kellie, just calm down. We'll take care of Fatty Patty.

(Justin, Keanu and Brad all end their phone calls and start texting.)

PATRICIA

Hey Brad… What's up, Keanu?… How's it going, Justin?

(Justin, Keanu and Brad all look up.)

JUSTIN

What?

KEANU

It's Fatty Patty.

BRAD

What a slut!

(The three boys go on texting and walk away. Another ringtone. Patricia takes out her phone. She checks to see who's calling.)

PATRICIA *(on the phone)*

Hi Kyle… Yes, I heard. It's no problem if you'd rather go to the dance with Kellie… Oh really?… You broke up with her? When?… Oh wow!… Just let me think about it, okay?… Can you call me tonight?… Fine. Talk to you later.

(Patricia puts away her phone and looks at the ground. Then she lifts her fist and quickly pulls it downward.)

PATRICIA *(with a "fist pump")*

YES!

SCENE 2   BE TRUE

(Paul is still sitting on a bench – stage right. Suddenly Liam and Noah approach him from stage left, passing Patricia as they cross the stage. They sit down on both sides of him. Paul looks up from his book.)

LIAM

Hey, you're Paul, aren't you?

PAUL

Yeah.

LIAM

We're in the same Phys Ed class.

PAUL

I know.

NOAH *(to Paul)*

You know me, too?

PAUL

Sure. You're Liam Ryan. We went to the same elementary school.

NOAH

Is that all you remember?

PAUL

No, I remember once on my way home from school in 5th grade that you and John Krabbenhoft offered me a cigarette.

NOAH

Geez, you remember that?

PAUL

Yeah, I think you guys had skipped school and smoked a bit.

NOAH

Hey, you got a good memory.

PAUL

I'll never forget it. You expected me to smoke the cigarette, but I was scared to, 'cause I'd never smoked before, and I remember the problems my dad had when he gave up smoking, so I put it in my pocket and said I'd smoke it later.

LIAM

And did you?

PAUL

Nope. I never even got the chance. I forgot it was in my pocket and wore a different pair of pants the next day.

NOAH

Did your parents find it?

PAUL

My mom did. The next day when she wanted to wash my pants.

LIAM

Did you get punished?

PAUL

Nope. When I came home from school the next day, my mom said she wouldn't tell my dad about the weed in my pocket if I promised never to smoke again. So I promised her.

NOAH

Speaking of weed, we got some really good Blue Dream here. Interested?

LIAM

Nice stuff. Mild and mellow, and it gives you a good high.

PAUL

Thanks, but I'm not into weed.

LIAM

Aw, c'mon, Paul. You'll go nuts. It'll change your whole perspective on life.

PAUL

Actually, I like the perspective I have on life without drugs.

NOAH

We'll give you a free sample.

PAUL

No, thanks. By the way, what time is it?

NOAH

Five o'clock, why?

PAUL

My mom's expecting me for early dinner. We have our family night at the movies tonight.

NOAH

So you're still a mama's boy?!

PAUL *(getting up from the bench and walking away)*

You bet. Mom's the best!

LIAM

I bet she still wipes your butt!

PAUL *(over his shoulder)*

No, to tell the truth, I just learned how to do it myself. See you around, guys.

(Paul walks towards center stage. Liam and Noah take out their reefers and start smoking as they walk off stage. Arriving at center stage, Paul runs into Ethan, Lucas and Logan who are laughing and staggering a bit. Ethan is holding a bottle of vodka which he offers to Paul.)

ETHAN

Hey, it's my old friend, Paul. Hey buddy, how about a swig?

PAUL

Hey Ethan, sorry, but no thanks. I gotta get home.

LUCAS

Aw, c'mon on, Paul. Just one for the road.

PAUL

No, Lucas. To tell the truth, I don't really like the stuff.

LOGAN

This is no stuff, man. This is vodka, pure and delicious. This is what real men drink.

(Ethan holds Paul and tries to force him to drink.)

ETHAN

Just one swig. You'll love it.

PAUL *(struggling to free himself)*

Let go, Ethan. I'm not kidding. I gotta go home.

(Logan and Lucas take hold of Paul from behind and force him to the ground.)

LOGAN

What's wrong? Is the little boy gonna be late for dinner?

LUCAS

How about a little cocktail before you go?

(Ethan takes out a funnel and sticks it in Paul's mouth. He is about to pour the vodka into the funnel when Amy and Holly show up on stage – stage right.)

AMY *(to Ethan)*

Hey there, big boy. Don't waste that good firewater on a little kid like that.

(Ethan, Logan and Lucas look up.)

HOLLY

Yeah, guys. We are two thirsty chicks with a cozy little party room in the basement.

AMY

Anybody up for a little fun?

HOLLY

My car's just around the corner.

LUCAS

Hey, cool. We'll be right with you.

LOGAN

Forget that jerk, Ethan. He isn't worth it.

ETHAN

You're right. Let's go.

(Ethan, Logan and Lucas head off to join Amy and Holly. Paul gets up and takes the funnel out of his mouth.)

PAUL

Hey Ethan, you forgot something.

ETHAN

Keep it. Where we're going, we don't need any toys.

(Ethan, Logan and Lucas join Amy and Holly. As Ethan offers Amy the bottle, she takes it and empties it on the ground.)

ETHAN

What're you doing?

(At the same time Amy and Holly take out their police badges.)

AMY

So, guys, just follow us to our party room.

HOLLY *(talking into a walkie-talkie)*

Three underage juveniles suspected of illegal alcohol consumption in public. Meet you at the squad car.

LOGAN

What? Who are you?

AMY

Special agents, vice squad.

HOLLY

It looks like you guys are going to spend the night in our little party room. Maybe you've heard of it before. We call it "the cell".

AMY *(calling over to Paul)*

Are you okay, Paul?

PAUL *(straightening his clothes)*

I'm fine, big sister. Thanks.

AMY

Sure thing. And tell Mom I'll be a bit late for dinner.

PAUL

You bet.

(Paul waves goodbye and walks off stage – stage left – while Amy, Holly, Ethan, Logan and Lucas walk off stage right.)

SCENE 3   OPEN YOUR EYES

*(A group of six students, Jake, Mike, Matt, Ben, Jade and Claire, arrives at center stage, every student carrying a chair. They form a semi-circle which is open to the audience, and then they sit down. As if on command, each student **except Jake** crosses their right leg. Then, again as if on command, each student **except Jake** crosses their arms. And finally each student **except Jake** bows their head and shakes it slowly – while Jake fidgets, slumps and seems uneasy. Suddenly Alexandra appears, and each student **except Jake** sits up straight with both feet squarely on the floor and their hands properly placed on their laps. Now Jake crosses his right leg, then he crosses his arms, bows his head and begins to shake it slowly. Alexandra is holding a clipboard. She glances at it.)*

ALEXANDRA *(looking around the semi-circle)*

 I think you all know why we have come together today.

(Each student except Jake nods.)

Our principal, Mr. Nau, has asked me as the student body president to select a group of qualified students to deal with a particular case of bullying that is disrupting school spirit and tarnishing our school's excellent reputation in the community.

(Mike raises his hand.)

ALEXANDRA

Yes, Mike?

MIKE

Excuse me, Alex, but can you tell us why we've been selected?

(Claire raises her hand.)

ALEXANDRA

Yes, Claire?

CLAIRE

Perhaps I can help you, Mike. Matt and I assisted Alex with the selection.

(Matt raises his hand.)

MATT *(taking out his clipboard)*

Yes, that's right. The three of us were given a list of students nominated by the school administration, students they thought were suitable to participate in this special committee.

CLAIRE *(taking out her clipboard)*

We were told that the members of the committee should be able to communicate honestly and seriously.

MATT

And they must be fair.

CLAIRE

They should be responsible, reliable and willing to find a way to control bullying.

MATT

They should also be able to deal calmly with conflicts.

ALEXANDRA

And they must be polite and able to work together with students who are not their friends. Does that answer your question, Mike?

MIKE

Yes, thank you, Alex.

ALEXANDRA

Fine. Now before we begin, Claire, Matt and I would like to briefly relate the events leading up to this meeting. Claire…

CLAIRE *(looks at her clipboard)*

It all began when Jake Griffith enrolled at our school three months ago.

(Jake moves around on his seat. He groans aloud, obviously uneasy.)

JAKE

Oh man…

CLAIRE *(pauses and stares at Jake, looks at her clipboard and reads:)*

"The first incident occurred on September 3rd, Jake Griffith's second day of school."

JAKE *(more to himself)*

Bullshit.

ALEXANDRA *(to Jake)*

Jake, would you please keep your comments to yourself.

(Jake gives her an evil look.)

CLAIRE *(continues reading)*

"After school Jake took a stick and rammed it between the spokes of four different bicycles that passed by him, causing the bikes to stop abruptly, so the students, who were all much younger than Jake, fell off and injured themselves. In one case a student was hospitalized with a broken wrist."

JAKE

They were all riding too fast on the sidewalk, so I decided to teach them a lesson.

ALEXANDRA

Excuse me, Jake, but you will have a chance to reply to the accusations once they have been presented. So, please, wait your turn...

(Mike raises his hand.)

MIKE

I was there when it happened. I witnessed the entire incident.

JAKE

Fake news!

MIKE

I was there, because I was going home with my younger sister who also got knocked off her bike. When I tried to stop Jake from attacking other kids, he hit me with his stick and called me a name before he ran off.

JAKE *(to Mike)*

Fake news! Fake news! Fake news!

MIKE

You're the one who's fake! Fake Jake!

JAKE

Shut up, prick!

ALEXANDRA

Quiet, please, all of you! Alright. Let's continue. Matt…

MATT *(reading from his clipboard)*

"The second incident occurred on the third day of school, September 4th. Jake approached three 10-year-old girls, all 5th graders, and showed them pornographic film clips.

(Ben raises his hand.)

ALEXANDRA

Yes, Ben?

BEN

I saw him with the girls. He was bent over his iPhone, showing them something, so I walked over to him and saw it was a very explicit porn clip. The girls were shocked.

JAKE

Aw, c'mon. I was just giving them a little sex education. It really made their day.

ALEXANDRA

Jake, I asked you to wait your turn, please.

JAKE *(to Alexandra)*

Screw you!

BEN

Shut up, Jake, or I'll shut you up!

(Jake stands up and walks over to Ben.)

JAKE

What're you gonna do about it, dude?

ALEXANDRA

Sit down, Jake, or we'll call security.

(Tension builds. After about five seconds Jake goes back to his seat and sits down.)

CLAIRE *(reading)*

"The third incident occurred on September 5th. Jake started to spread several false rumors on WhatsApp."

JAKE

Hey baby, fake news is the spice of life.

ALEXANDRA

This is your last warning, Jake. Either wait your turn, or we'll carry on this meeting without you.

(A short pause.)

ALEXANDRA

Claire, would you please tell us what the rumors were about?

CLAIRE *(reading)*

One rumor claimed that Student A was a junky, which isn't true. Another rumor said that Student B had poisoned his parents when he was twelve, and that isn't true either.

MATT

"Another rumor claimed that Student C was working after school as a hooker, which isn't true."

(Jade raises her hand.)

JADE

Just so everybody knows, I am Student C. Jake spread the rumor that I was selling my body online. He even tried to set up a fake website with photoshopped pornographic pictures of me.

(Jake shakes his head.)

ALEXANDRA *(to Jade)*

Thank you, Jade. I know how difficult the whole situation was for you.

JADE *(almost breaks down, wipes her eyes)*

The whole school thought I was a prostitute, and my boss at the flower shop found out about it and fired me, even though I explained it to him. And my parents' friends basically stopped talking to them.

ALEXANDRA *(consoling Jade)*

Thank you, Jade, for helping us understand the serious aftereffects of that rumor. Would you like to step outside for a moment?

(Jade shakes her head. She is obviously choked up.)

ALEXANDRA

Alright. Matt, would you continue, please?

MATT

"A fourth rumor claimed that our principal, Mr. Nau, was a member of Vanguard America, a white supremacist, racist, neo-Nazi, neo-fascist organization. A picture of Mr. Nau was photoshopped into a rally organized by Vanguard America. As a matter of fact, Mr. Nau has nothing to do with Nazis at all."

ALEXANDRA *(not reading)*

And a fifth rumor said that I was pregnant, but I'm not.

JAKE

You sure look pregnant. Or are you always that fat?

JADE *(jumping up to defend Alexandra)*

Who do you think you are, calling Alexandra fat? She's one of the most beautiful and slender girls in the class, dickhead!

JAKE *(also jumping up)*

Red card! Penalty! Foul! Call the cops! That girl used a bad word! I'm gonna tell the principal, and you'll be in big trouble, bitch!

BEN *(jumps up and threatens Jake)*

Watch out who you call a bitch! Jade is my girlfriend, and…

JAKE *(grins cynically at Ben)*

Oh, isn't that sweet! Big Ben is standing up for that little slut he calls his girlfriend.

BEN *(rushing over to confront Jake)*

Listen here, you little prick…

JAKE *(holding up his hands)*

Don't touch me, or I'll call Mr Nau… NOW!

(At that moment Alexandra's phone rings. Everyone freezes.)

ALEXANDRA

Excuse me.

(She puts her phone to her ear.)

ALEXANDRA

Alexandra speaking…

(She quickly glances at Jake.)

ALEXANDRA

Yes, Mr. Nau. We're still discussing the matter… Alright.

(Silence. Everyone in the group is curious.)

ALEXANDRA

Hello, Ms. Griffith. Thank you for coming to school today. I understand you're in Mr. Nau's office right now.

(Jake looks startled. He sits down. Ben also sits down. Jake begins to shake his head.)

ALEXANDRA

We are in the middle of our discussion. If you don't mind, I'll put you on speaker.

(Jake shakes his head and looks even more upset. Alexandra puts her phone on speaker and holds it up, so everyone can hear it.)

MS GRIFFITH *(off stage)*

Hi, Jake. I know this must be a shock for you, since you haven't seen me for nearly five years. But the school got in touch with me, 'cause they said they're about to kick you out 'cause of some stuff you did. So they asked me to talk to you, 'cause they want to give you one more chance… Are you listening to me, Jake?

JAKE *(shaking his head in disbelief)*

Get lost! Get outta my life! Leave me alone, damn it!

MS GRIFFITH *(off stage)*

I know you must hate me, and I can understand why.

JAKE

You left me and Dad without even saying goodbye.

MS GRIFFITH *(off stage)*

I didn't have time…

JAKE

You didn't have time? Don't give me that bullshit! I was your child! Just ten years old! Your only child!

MS GRIFFITH *(off stage)*

I couldn't go on living the life I was living. I had to leave.

JAKE

What do you mean? You had to leave?

MS GRIFFITH *(off stage)*

My world was dark and frightening, and your father…

JAKE

Don't mention my father!

MS GRIFFITH *(off stage)*

He didn't understand, and he…

JAKE

Shut up! Shut up!

MS GRIFFITH *(off stage)*

I'd like to tell you about it later when we're alone…

JAKE

No way! Get out of here! Get out of my life! I never wanna see you again!

(He gets up and walks over to Alexandra, threateningly.)

JAKE

Turn that thing off before I smash it to smithereens!

(Alexandra hangs up and puts the phone down. Silence. Then suddenly…)

JAKE *(screaming)*

Ahh!

(Jake drops to his knees and pounds his fists on the floor.)

JAKE

No! No! No!

(Then he lowers his head to his thighs and buries it under his arms. Alexandra gets up and walks over to Jake. She stands above him for a moment, then she hesitantly crouches down to his level. She carefully puts a hand on his back and waits. After about five seconds she says:)

ALEXANDRA *(cautiously)*

Jake, what can we do for you?

(No answer. Five more seconds.)

ALEXANDRA *(a bit louder)*

Jake, is there anything we can do for you?

(Jake slowly lifts his head. He wipes his eyes with his hand, then he wipes his nose with his sleeve.)

JAKE *(almost whispering)*

Help me…

(Jake raises his head to look at the ceiling. He sighs, then he looks at the audience.)

JAKE *(louder, imploring)*

Help me, please!

SCENE 4 BE YOURSELF

(Chris is sitting behind a table – stage left – putting on makeup and jewelry.)

CHRIS

Until I was about five or six I didn't know if I was a girl or a boy. I remember a teacher yelling at me for going to the toilet with the girls. That's when I realized I was different from other guys. Starting on my 8th birthday, I wouldn't let anyone cut my hair. I kept growing it until I was fourteen, so it got really long. Kids would often threaten me after school and yell things. During lunch breaks there were kids who pushed me around a lot, they even bullied me in class when the teacher wasn't looking, 'cause they said I acted like a girl, or I didn't like sports, or 'cause my hair was so long. At first they called me a sissy or a pussy and later all sorts of names like "ladyboy" or "shemale" or "tranny", and they pushed me around a lot. I wasn't quite sure what all the words really meant, so I googled them and checked on YouTube. I think I was just looking for something I could call myself, some kind of identity. I knew how I felt, but I didn't know what to call it. Then one day I came across the words TRANSGENDER PRIDE, and I said "that's it"! That explains everything: I'm transgender.

I've always been fascinated with women. As a kid I was just crazy about women's bathing suits, I always wanted to put one on. In fact, I did it once at a friend's house. His sister wore the same size as me, so I snuck into her room and tried on her one-piece swimming suit. I quickly glanced at myself in the mirror before I panicked and ripped it off. I was really afraid of being caught, especially because I felt I was born with a secret, although I didn't quite know what that secret was.

Sometimes I still stuff a pillow in my shirt and pretend I'm pregnant. I stand sideways in front of a mirror and take selfies.

I love shopping and cross-dressing, and my collection of women's shoes keeps getting bigger.

I never actually told my family I'm transgender. I never said, "Hey guys, I'm not really a boy." But my mom asked me when I was around 15. "Are you?" And I said, "Yeah." You only feel you're not normal if you're treated that way. Us trans people are actually normal people. We have ideals, we want to be happy and respected.

People who don't know me probably don't want to meet me, but when they get to know me, they understand who I am. A lot of people think that we decide to be trans. But it's not a choice. Nothing makes you trans. You're just born that way. So you have to learn to accept it for yourself. And once you've accepted it, you have to hope that society around you will accept it, but that's the hardest part, because you can't <u>make</u> people accept you.

Just last week a person I know from my Transgender Pride group was attacked on his way home from the weekly meeting, and…

(At that moment, a person wearing a hooded sweatshirt appears on stage – from stage left – and stands directly in front of Chris with their back to the audience. We can't exactly see what they are doing, but they seem to be interacting with Chris. After about 10 seconds, the person scurries off stage – stage right – holding up their middle finger to the audience. Chris stands up. The makeup on his/her face has been smeared, and he/she is now holding a large manila envelope that wasn't there before. Chris takes a letter out of the envelope and begins to read:)

CHRIS *(reading)*

"Hey, tranny, or whatever you call yourself: pansy, girlie man, genderbender, ladyboy. In my opinion you're nothin' but a freak, a fucking gay faggot, a trandgender fake who just says he's a girl, so he can have sex with other dudes. You're a damn liar and a sick son-of-a-bitch. Filth like you should be burned alive or cut up into a million pieces and thrown to the dogs. Don't you know? Boys are boys, and girls are girls. You can't change your sex… We're gonna get you one of these nights. Us decent dudes are gonna beat the shit outta you with our baseball bats before we chop you up and douse you with gasoline. By the time we're through with you, you'll be on your knees begging us to light that match and burn the hell outta ya. My dad even said we should bury you up to the neck and run over your head with a lawnmower, but I don't wanna mess up my new shoes. See you soon, the Tranny Killers."

(Chris looks up at the audience. He smiles. Then he tears up the letter and says:)

CHRIS

"The Tranny Killers!" How original.

(He chuckles, picks up a mirror and takes a look.)

Well, well, I think I could use some new makeup.

(Chris winks at the audience and waves as he heads off stage.)

SCENE 5   STAND UP

(Speaker 1, female, walks past the audience, hesitates, goes back and stands in front of a member of the audience.)

SPEAKER 1

Hey, I remember you back in elementary school. You were on the school bus, weren't you? I'll never forget the time me and a couple other kids were sitting behind you in the back of the bus, and we threw pieces of bubble gum into your hair. It was so funny. You didn't even notice it until you got off the bus, and you reached back and felt it. The look on your face was a real killer. There must have been at least 20 pieces of gum stuck to your hair. You started tugging away at it, trying to pull it off, but the more you pulled, the worse it got. And the best part was that the next day your hair was real short, so I figure your mom had to cut all the gum out.

(Speaker 1 chuckles and takes a few steps back. At the same time, Speaker 3, male, walks past the audience in front of Speaker 1, hesitates, goes back and stands in front of another member of the audience – female.)

SPEAKER 2

I don't believe it. You mean, it's really you? After all I did to you. I thought you'd killed yourself years ago. Online suicide or something.

(He changes his voice to mock the person who was bullied and committed suicide.)

"I hope you never forgive yourself and never forget my name. You'll have blood on your hands for as long as you live."

(He reflects for a moment.)

Wait a minute. It can't be... You really did kill yourself, didn't you? How could I forget? You're not... Yeah, sure. You're her sister, aren't you? It's amazing. You look just like her. No offense, but you guys could be twins. It's those genes, you know. By the way, speaking of jeans, I was the one who got her to drop her jeans and take those nude Instagram pics. You guys were new at school, what we used to call "fresh meat", and I acted like I was interested in her and told her to send me some really sexy pics. I mean, I didn't make her do it. I just said, if she didn't do it, there were lots of other girls who would, so if she wanted to be my girlfriend… I mean. How stupid can you be! I hardly knew her, but she sent those pics and within two days they were all over school. Everybody was talking about her, saying stuff like: "Did you see those creepy pictures? – What a slut!" I even saw some older girls spit at her and kick her when she walked down the hall.

(He hesitates, looks more intensely at the member of the audience.)

Hey, what's your name?

(He holds his hand to his ear to symbolize a phone call)

Give me your number, and I'll get in touch.

(Speaker 2 winks at the member of the audience and steps back. At the same time, Speaker 3, female, and Speaker 4, female, walk past the audience in front of Speaker 2, hesitate, go back and stand in front of another member of the audience – male.)

SPEAKER 3

Hey you!

(Speaker 3 points at the male in the audience.)

You thought you were his friend, didn't you?

(Speaker 3 gives the audience member a strange look.)

SPEAKER 4

But you had no clue, did you? You thought you were standing up for that retard, didn't you? But you're even more of an idiot than he is. You know, we never would have touched you if you hadn't stood up for that jerk.

SPEAKER 3

We were just having fun with him. We always had fun with him. And he loved it. We could punch him in the face or kick him in the head, and he'd just laugh about it.

SPEAKER 4

I'll never forget when we told him to walk across the frozen pond in the winter, and he broke through the ice at least five times.

SPEAKER 3

His lips turned blue, and he couldn't stop shivering, so we set his jacket on fire and told him to put it on, so he could warm up, but he burned his hands and started crying. So we just left him there.

SPEAKER 4

The next day his hands were bandaged, but he asked us if we could go to the pond again sometime.

SPEAKER 3

And then you came along, Mr. Super Hero.

SPEAKER 4

You thought you were helping him, but you just totally messed things up.

SPEAKER 3

He loved playing Indians with us when we tied him to a tree and tickled him.

SPEAKER 4

And we pulled his pants down and started to play with his you-know-what.

SPEAKER 3

And then you came along and tried to free him.

SPEAKER 4

That really pissed me off which is why I cracked your head with that branch.

SPEAKER 3

And then we kicked the shit out of you.

(Speakers 3 and 4 look at each other, nod and step back. Suddenly we hear a voice from the audience.)

SPEAKER 5 *(blows a whistle, then stands up in the audience)*
Attention!
(The first four speakers stand at attention!)
SPEAKER 6 *(blows a whistle, then stands up in the audience)*
Forward march!
(The first four speakers march forward – about five steps.)
SPEAKER 7 *(blows a whistle, then stands up in the audience)*
Halt!
(The first four speakers stop. Speakers 5, 6 and 7 approach the first four speakers. For a short moment Speakers 5, 6 and 7 stand in front of Speakers 1, 2, 3 and 4, staring at them with their backs to the audience: Speaker 5 in front of Speaker 1, Speaker 6 in front of Speaker 2, Speaker 7 in front of Speakers 3 and 4. Then Speakers 5, 6 and 7 turn around and face the audience as they begin to speak in unison.)
SPEAKERS 5, 6 and 7 *(in unison)*
We were bystanders. We didn't do a thing!
(Speaker 5 spreads their legs, as Speaker 1 goes down on her hands and knees and crawls halfway through the opening made by the legs, her head is down.)
SPEAKER 5 *(looking down at Speaker 1)*
I saw you throw the gum at that kid, and I wanted to say something. You were always bullying other kids on the bus.
SPEAKER 1 *(looking up from between the legs)*
But you were scared of me, weren't you? You knew what I'd do, didn't you? Because you knew what I did to all those other kids.
(Speaker 5 sits down on Speaker 1's back.)
SPEAKER 1
Ah!
(Speaker 6 spreads their legs, as Speaker 2 goes down on his hands and knees and crawls halfway through the opening made by the legs, his head is down.)

SPEAKER 6

I felt so sorry for that girl when the nude pictures of her showed up on Instagram. She was new, and I kind of liked her. Maybe she'd still be alive if I'd talked to her.

SPEAKER 2 *(looking up from between the legs)*

But you were scared of what people would say if they knew you were friends with that slut. By the way, I have some pretty wicked pictures of you when you were at Aaron's party.

(Speaker 5 sits down on Speaker 2's back.)

SPEAKER 2

Ah!

(Speaker 7 spreads their legs, as Speaker 3 goes down on her hands and knees and crawls halfway through the opening made by the legs, his head is down. Speaker 4 goes down on her hands and knees and also crawls halfway through the opening made by the legs, her head is down, too.)

SPEAKER 7 *(looking down at Speakers 3 and 4)*

I knew what you guys were doing to that autistic kid, but I didn't know what to do.

SPEAKER 3 *(looking up from between the legs)*

'cause you're chicken shit. You're a yellow-bellied coward.

SPEAKER 7

Sure, I was afraid you'd crack my head like you did with Greg when he tried to stop you.

SPEAKER 4 *(looking up from between the legs)*

It was none of Greg's business. We were having fun with that retard, and he had no right to stop us.

(Speaker 7 sits down on Speakers 3 and 4.)

SPEAKERS 3 and 4 *(in unison)*

Ouch!

(Speakers 1, 2, 3 and 4 begin crawling around in a circle for about ten seconds, moaning – with the bystanders still on their backs. While

crawling, they first speak in a low voice but keep getting louder until they are shouting, not necessarily in unison.)

SPEAKERS 1, 2, 3 and 4

Get off my back! Get off my back! Get off my back! Get off my back! Get off my back! Get off my back!...

SPEAKER 7 *(blows a whistle)*

Stand up!

(All seven speakers stand up.)

SPEAKER 5 *(blows a whistle)*

Attention!

(All seven speakers get in line next to each other, facing the audience. They stand at attention.)

SPEAKER 6 *(blows a whistle)*

Forward march!

(All seven speakers march forward – about five steps.)

SPEAKER 7 *(blows a whistle)*

Halt! Stop!

SPEAKER 1

What for?

SPEAKER 6

You bully other kids, don't you?

SPEAKER 1

Yeah. That's how my parents brought me up. My dad beat me with his belt and chained me to the garage door, so I went up and down when he opened and shut it. I felt like shit, so I wanted somebody else to feel like shit.

SPEAKER 5

And does it make you feel better?

SPEAKER 2

What?

SPEAKER 2

Bullying other kids?

SPEAKER 1

You mean when I make them feel like shit?

SPEAKER 6

Yeah.

SPEAKER 2

At first it makes me feel like I'm better than the other kid. When I see a girl get scared, when I know I can get her to do anything I want, it makes me feel real strong.

SPEAKER 6

How do you feel when you go home?

SPEAKER 3

Like shit, 'cause I know my stepdad hates me, and he's gonna make me feel like I'm just garbage. He yells at me all the time, and my mom never stands up for me. I know she feels bad when he treats me like that, but she doesn't say anything. She even tells him when I do something wrong, so he can punch me in the stomach again.

SPEAKER 7

Do you think your parents are right to treat you bad?

SPEAKER 4

I'm just no good, so I guess they gotta treat me bad.

SPEAKER 6

Nobody has a right to treat you bad!

SPEAKER 3

The only time other kids are nice to me is when I scare them.

SPEAKER 5

Do you think they'll like you if you scare them?

SPEAKER 2

Nobody likes me.

SPEAKER 1

Nobody likes me either.

SPEAKER 3

I don't really have any friends except for... what's her name.

(She nods at Speaker 4.)

SPEAKER 4

Don't look at me. I just hang out with you, 'cause I got nobody else to hang out with.

SPEAKER 5

Hey, I imagine you're going through a difficult time. You know, we all have our troubles. Maybe we should sit down and talk sometime.

SPEAKER 1 *(turns her head towards Speaker 5 and stares)*

What?

SPEAKER 6

I know bullying gives you this "high" and makes you feel almighty and powerful. But the truth is, a few years from now when you grow up, you will just look in the mirror and feel sad.

SPEAKER 2 *(turns his head towards Speaker 6 and stares)*

What?

SPEAKER 7

I have a black belt in judo and karate, and I'm a state champion in kick boxing. I could beat the shit outta both of you in seconds if I wanted to.

SPEAKERS 3 and 4 *(turn their heads towards Speaker 7 and stare)*

So what?

SPEAKERS 5, 6 and 7 *(stare back at the bullies)*

Why don't you guys just say you're sorry?

(Speakers 1, 2, 3 and 4 start repeating the word "sorry" as they get down on their hands and knees again and crawl away.)

SPEAKERS 1, 2, 3 and 4

Sorry, sorry, sorry, sorry…

(Speakers 5, 6 and 7 watch Speakers 1, 2, 3 and 4 crawl off stage.)

SPEAKER 6 *(looks at Speakers 5 and 7)*

They didn't mean it, did they?

(Speakers 7 and 8 shake their heads.)

SPEAKER 7 *(looks at Speakers 5 and 6)*
They're never going to change, are they?
(Speakers 5 and 6 shake their heads.)
SPEAKER 5 *(looks at Speakers 6 and 7)*
But at least we tried, didn't we?
SPEAKERS 5, 6 and 7 *(look at the audience, hesitate for a moment, then in unison)*
Sorry!

SCENE 6   SORRY, I CAN'T

(Music. A young girl dances onto the stage with a suitcase. For ten seconds. Then the music abruptly stops and the girl freezes in an extremely awkward pose. She looks at the audience and puts the suitcase on the floor.)

CYNTHIA

When I was 14 years old I was one of the best dancers in America… and then I became a full-time student at Dance Academy. I live here. I go to school here. I dance here. And I eat here… sometimes.

(The music continues. Cynthia goes on dancing. For ten seconds. Then once again the music abruptly stops and she freezes in another extremely awkward pose.)

CYNTHIA

After two years something happened. Inside me. And I slowly became a sadly overweight and smelly dancer who was never going to be a star at the greatest dance company in America, the American Ballet Theater.

(The music continues. Cynthia goes on dancing. For ten seconds. Then once again the music abruptly stops and she freezes in another extremely awkward pose.)

CYNTHIA

My dream died with every chocolate donut I stuffed in my face.
(We hear the crack of a whip. Cynthia stands up straight, hesitates, then addresses the audience again.)

CYNTHIA

My name is Cynthia Jordan, Cindy for short. And I am my own worst bully.
(Cynthia is approached from behind by Sarah Black, dressed in black leather, dancing, holding a whip.)

SARAH BLACK *(cracks the whip, loud, aggressive)*

This is what it's like to attend the best dance college in America. Your body will be challenged all day, every day.

(Sarah Black cracks the whip.)

CYNTHIA

My dance classes are intense. They make me use every single muscle in my body.

SARAH BLACK *(cracks the whip again, loud, flamboyant)*

You are so lucky to be here. It's every girl's dream. The greatest dance school in America. The chance to be a star.

(Sarah Black cracks the whip, aggressive)

But you're getting fat!

(Sarah Black cracks the whip.)

You're slowing down.

(Sarah Black cracks the whip, makes a dramatic gesture.)

You must move like a swan, not like a slug. Jump like a gazelle. Not like a pig.

(Sarah Black cracks the whip.)

Take these pills!

(Sarah Black cracks the whip and throws imaginary pills at Cynthia.)

And stop eating breakfast, for God's sake! You look like a slob! A pig! Oink, oink, oink!

(Sarah Black lets out a snide laugh and dances away. Cynthia looks at the audience, almost pleading.)

CYNTHIA

Hey, I've already stopped eating lunch!

(The music again. Cynthia dances. For ten seconds. Then the music abruptly stops and she freezes in another awkward pose.)

CYNTHIA

In a program like this, I am constantly reminded how lucky I am to be here, how every young dancer wants to be here, and they make me feel like: "I can't leave. If I leave, I'm nobody. I just have to work harder and harder and do what they say."

(The music again. Cynthia dances. For ten seconds. Then the music abruptly stops and she freezes in another extremely awkward pose.)

CYNTHIA

When I started binge eating, it was just energy bars and healthy stuff at first. I couldn't stop myself. I felt really bad about it, 'cause my teachers were trying to make me one of the best dancers ever, so I stuck my finger down my throat and tried to get rid of everything. But then the urge to eat was even stronger.

(Cynthia is approached from the side by someone who looks like a fat fairy, she pretends to be stuffing food in her face.)

FAT FAIRY

Yummy, try this.

(The fat fairy holds out an imaginary piece of food.)

You'll love it.

(The fat fairy sticks her hand in Cynthia's face.)

Take a bite. It's so good.

(Cynthia takes an imaginary bite. The fat fairy does a little fat fairy dance.)

FAT FAIRY

Yummy, isn't it?

(Cynthia stuffs more and more of the imaginary food in her mouth.)

FAT FAIRY *(rubbing her hand all over Cynthia's face.)*

More, more, more…

(Cynthia tries to ward off the fat fairy.)

Stop it! Stop it!

FAT FAIRY *(stops rubbing Cynthia's face)*

Aw, does Cindy have a tummy ache?

(Suddenly the fat fairy backs away from Cindy. Appalled. She waves her hand in front of her nose and cries out.)

FAT FAIRY

Ugh! What's that awful smell?

(Still waving her hand in front of her nose.)

FAT FAIRY

Did you just…? Ugh! Pew, pew, that stinks! Like rotten eggs! I'm outta here!

(The fat fairy runs off.)

CYNTHIA

I eat, because I'm hungry. And because of the feelings. Bad feelings. Black feelings. But when I stuff myself, it's like talking to an old friend. The more I stuff myself, the better I feel. I can eat more boxes of cereal and more tubs of ice cream and more candy and more bags of potato chips in one evening than most people eat in a month. And afterwards…

(Cynthia does a little awkward dance and falls.)

Afterwards I feel worse than before. And the gas pains…

(A boy, Ryan, approaches Cynthia from the side. Hip-hop style, a cool way of walking, holding a grocery bag.)

RYAN

Hey Cindy! Hungry?

CYNTHIA *(getting up)*

Yes, no, I'm starving, but sorry, I can't…

RYAN *(pulling a snack out of his bag)*

Hey, how about this stuff?

CYNTHIA

No, sorry, I can't.

RYAN *(pulling another snack out of his bag)*

And some of this? You normally love it?

CYNTHIA

Sorry, I can't.

RYAN

C'mon, you're always crazy about it.

CYNTHIA

Not today.

RYAN

You want anything else? I'm on my way to the store.

CYNTHIA

That's really nice of you, Ryan, but no, sorry, I can't.

RYAN

Well, okay, but gimme a call if you change your mind..

CYNTHIA

Sure.

(A telephone rings. Cynthia takes out her cell phone and answers it.)

CYNTHIA

Hi, this is Cindy. *(listening)* Yes, Aunt Carol. My suitcase is packed, and I'm outside the main hall. *(listening)* Okay, see you in about five minutes.

(Cynthia hangs up and looks at the audience.)

Yeah, it wasn't easy explaining to Mom and Dad that I was leaving Dance Academy, especially after all the money they invested in my training here, but I think they kind of understand.

(Ryan, the hip-hop boy, approaches Cynthia from the other side, holding a second bag.)

RYAN

Hey Cindy, why the suitcase?

CYNTHIA

I'm leaving, Ryan.

RYAN

For the weekend?

CYNTHIA

For good.

RYAN

Too bad. Gonna miss you.

CYNTHIA

Gonna miss you, too.

RYAN

Something wrong?

CYNTHIA

I'm getting fat.

RYAN

I understand.

(Ryan hesitates for a moment and pats his own stomach.)

RYAN *(offering Cynthia his two bags)*

Sure you don't want anything for the road? I got more than enough.

CYNTHIA *(patting her stomach)*

No, sorry, I can't.

(A car horn can be heard, and Cindy runs off. Ryan goes on munching his snack and walks off stage.)

SCENE 7   SHARING

(A telephone rings. Five times. Jackie appears on stage and stands in front of the audience. She is holding a phone. She dials a number, and the same ringtone as before is heard. She lets it ring six times. Sandy appears on stage behind Jackie, she struggles to get her phone out of her pocket. It stops ringing before she is able to answer it. Once again Jackie dials a number. The same ringtone is heard. This time Sandy answers the phone immediately.)

SANDY

Hello, this is Sandy from the Samaritans. How can I help you?

(Jackie hangs up. She turns sideways. Sandy walks over to the backside of Jackie, she also turns sideways but facing the opposite direction – standing back-to-back with Jackie.)

Hello?

(Jackie shakes her head and dials a number. The same ringtone is heard. Sandy lets it ring three times. Then she answers the phone.)

Hello, this is Sandy from the Samaritans. Is there anything I can do for you?

JACKIE *(hesitantly)*

This is Jackie.

SANDY

Hello, Jackie. My name is Sandy. I work for the Samaritans. Is there any way I can help you?

(Sandy waits for an answer.)

Are you still there, Jackie?

(Sandy waits for an answer.)

JACKIE *(hesitant, almost whispering)*

Yes.

SANDY

Would you like to talk?

JACKIE

I'm not sure.

SANDY

Would you like me to talk a bit?

JACKIE

Yes.

SANDY

Like I said, my name is Sandy, and you have reached the Samaritan's Teen Hotline.

JACKIE

Are you a volunteer?

SANDY

Yes, I am. I work two or three shifts a week.

JACKIE

Do you get paid for doing what you're doing?

SANDY

No, volunteers never get paid.

JACKIE

So what do you do it for?

SANDY

What do I do what for?

JACKIE

Why do you sit around listening to other people talk about wanting to kill themselves? Does it turn you on?

(Jackie waits for an answer.)

Are you still there, Sandy?

SANDY

Yeah, I'm still here.

JACKIE

Why don't you answer my question?

(Jackie waits for an answer.)

SANDY

Because I wasn't sure if I could be honest.

JACKIE

What do you mean?

SANDY

Yes.

JACKIE

Yes what?

SANDY

Yes, it turns me on to listen to people talk about wanting to kill themselves.

JACKIE

What?

SANDY

You heard what I said. I love it when people tell me how bad life is and how there's no way out but to kill themselves.

JACKIE

I don't believe it.

SANDY

Why else do you think I'd sit here two or three times a week for hours and listen to all these depressing stories?

JACKIE

Are you sick?

SANDY

No.

JACKIE

Sure, you're sick.

SANDY

No, I'm quite normal actually.

JACKIE

Delighting in other people's misfortune? You call that normal?

SANDY

Sure, because it makes me feel normal.

JACKIE

What are you talking about?

SANDY

My middle name is misfortune.

JACKIE

I have no idea what you're talking about.

SANDY

All the sad stories I listen to are actually my story.

JACKIE

Your story?

SANDY

It turns me on, as you say, to listen to other people's sad stories, because I realize I'm not alone.

JACKIE

What do you mean?

SANDY

Want to hear my story?

(Sandy waits for an answer.)

Still there, Jackie?

JACKIE

Yeah…

SANDY

Well?

JACKIE

Yes.

SANDY

Want me to share my story?

JACKIE

Yes.

SANDY

The first time I tried to kill myself I was fifteen.

JACKIE

Fifteen?

SANDY

Yeah, I mean, I didn't really want to die. I just wanted to kill the way I felt, the darkness, the loneliness, the sadness.

JACKIE

Depression?

SANDY

Worse.

JACKIE

You felt worthless?

SANDY

Worse.

JACKIE

Like everything was fake?

SANDY

Exactly.

JACKIE

And there was no way anybody could love you, because everything you did or said was fake and disgusting?

SANDY

Right.

JACKIE

And you couldn't stand the way you looked?

SANDY

That's when I took my mom's sleeping pills.

JACKIE

How many?

SANDY

More than enough.

JACKIE

Why didn't you die?

SANDY

My brother found me pretty quick. And they pumped my stomach. It was awful.

JACKIE

That was the first time?

SANDY

The second time was a year later.

JACKIE

Didn't you see a therapist?

SANDY

Sure, but I just couldn't get rid of the feeling that the world would be better off without me.

JACKIE

Wasn't there anybody else you could talk to?

SANDY

Yeah, a girl.

JACKIE

A friend?

SANDY

Sometimes.

JACKIE

What did you tell her?

SANDY

She asked about the scars on my arms.

JACKIE

Oh yeah?

SANDY

I told her about the voices in my head that wouldn't stop.

JACKIE

I know what you mean.

SANDY

And that I just wanted to disappear.

JACKIE

Yeah…

SANDY

After that she always seemed busy when I called. Distant.

JACKIE

Really far away, right?

SANDY

Yeah.

JACKIE

What was your second attempt like?

SANDY

I went to a busy train station.

JACKIE

Did you jump?

SANDY

No, I was standing on the platform. Really scared. Shaking. Uncontrollably. When I caught a glimpse of the train driver and suddenly thought about how horrible he would feel…

JACKIE

And you didn't jump?

SANDY

I broke down and started crying.

JACKIE

Did people just walk by and ignore you?

SANDY

I don't remember. I had no idea. But suddenly this guy stopped and talked to me. He took me home and gave me a number to call.

JACKIE

What number?

SANDY

This number. I called this number, and a girl with a soft voice answered.

JACKIE

What did you say?

SANDY

I was all choked up. I wasn't totally sure why I was calling, but I told her I was thinking about suicide.

JACKIE

How did she react?

SANDY

She said there was no pressure to say anything. She explained that she would act as a pair of ears for me. It was just between her and me.

JACKIE

And what happened?

SANDY

I told her lots of stuff, and she said she was glad I told her.

JACKIE

Oh yeah?

SANDY

And she asked me why I wanted to die.

JACKIE

She did?

SANDY

I told her how I felt and what I thought and that sometimes I feel like something is pushing me over the edge.

JACKIE

I know that feeling.

SANDY

And she said, when you feel like that, just give it one more hour, one more day. Just wait a bit.

JACKIE

Oh yeah?

SANDY

And that's now my mantra: Just one more day.

JACKIE

Okay.

SANDY

And after I hung up, I went outside, and there was this dog just hanging around. I'd never seen him before. An ugly mutt. And he looked at me and then brushed his snout against my leg, as if to say: "I know how you feel. Could you scratch me behind the ears?"

(Sandy and Jackie slowly turn around to face each other. They hesitate. Then they gently hug each other for a moment, and Jackie says:)

JACKIE

I know how you feel.

(Sandy touches Jackie behind the ears, the two girls look at each other and smile.)

SCENE 8   SPEAK UP

(Ron stands at a lectern in front of the audience. He is the valedictorian of his graduating class, and he is at the end of his valedictory speech.)

RON

Before I conclude my speech, I would like to honor a student who isn't with us today, a student who didn't survive the battlefield we call school, a kid who was somehow different and didn't quite fit in. He was a nice guy, very sensitive and very artistic. He loved basketball, reading, painting and his cats Black and White. In a certain way, he had always been teased by other kids, but it wasn't until he turned 15 that the bullying pushed Tom to a point of no return. It all started at elementary school. When he was in 3rd grade a boy stabbed him several times in the arm with a sharp pencil. In 4th grade two girls banged his head against the wall when he went to the bathroom. In 6th grade other guys started calling him gay, because he wasn't the typical kind of 6th-grade boy. And that's when the cyber-bullying began. Taunts and rumors and photoshopped pictures. It was a very painful experience for Tom. It even got so bad that boys at school refused to sit next to him for fear he might touch them. A week after he turned 15, a group of younger boys set fire to him. After spraying him with an aerosol can they threw matches at him until he caught fire. The attack was recorded on a cell phone and posted on the Internet. Later that night he took his own life. We all knew what was going on. We knew who shoved him around and kicked him. We knew who locked him in a toilet stall and doused him with water. We knew who held his head in a toilet bowl. We knew who burned him. So why didn't we do anything? Because we thought someone else would do something about it. I wish I could tell Tom I'm sorry. I never actually took part in the bullying, but if you don't try to stop it, you're part of the problem. When an adult bullies a child, we call it abuse. When one kid does it to another kid, we say it's normal. Victims of bullying are often told to develop a thick skin, as if it is their own fault for being bullied. But what is going on right now in our schools, in our society, is not just teasing. Kids are threatening each other. Dangerously. And some teachers actually support this hate culture with their own fears of homosexuals, Muslims, Jews, Blacks, Hispanics, Asians and students who are somehow different. It is time we realized that bullying is not a "normal" part of the school experience. It is time we did more to stop bullies who humiliate, frighten and hurt others. And it is time to open the eyes of teachers, parents and students that what is going on in our hallowed halls is child-on-child abuse. We all have a moral responsibility to report child abuse to the proper authorities and to make schools a safe place for the "victims" and not a place of constant fear. It's too late for Tom, but it's not too late for thousands of victims whose lives are in danger every day. It was Tom's mother who found him after he had hanged himself from the overhead fan. My mother. Tom was my twin brother, my own twin brother had taken his life. My brother was gone. My wonderful brother is gone. And I did nothing to save him. I did nothing to protect him. I had always imagined us standing here together at graduation, the two of us, but now I stand here alone. I am the valedictorian, the top student of this class, and I am ashamed, because I didn't stand up for my brother. I lost him, and now I feel lost myself.

THE END

ABOUT THE AUTHOR

John Reed Middleton was born in Cedar Rapids, Iowa (USA).
He was a teacher for 43 years at a German school in Hamburg
where he taught English, Drama and Art. He has also spent
over 35 years subtitling films and translating screenplays
(www.middleton-group-translations.com).
During the past 30 years he has performed his own five one-act
plays (DAVID, THE DEATH OF A CLOWN, CARNIVAL AT
CASTLE ROCK, KILLING DADDY, LITTLE GOETHE and
DAS KLEID) at small theaters in and around Hamburg.

THE PLAYLET SERIES is his latest writing project, topical
collections of scenes in English for English learners from Year 1
to Year 12 (Level 1 to Level 6) who want to perform (english-
playlets.com).

By purchasing the play, you automatically obtain the stage
rights.